The Warlock of Sharrador

by

Gardner F. Fox

The Warlock of Sharrador
by Gardner F. Fox

Copyright © 2024

All Rights reserved.

ISBN: 978-93-68097-23-5

Published by

DOUBLE 9 BOOKS

2/13-B, Ansari Road
Daryaganj, New Delhi – 110002
info@double9books.com
www.double9books.com
Tel. 011-40042856

This book is under public domain

ABOUT THE AUTHOR

Gardner F. Fox (1911-1986) was a prolific American writer renowned for his contributions to the genres of fantasy, science fiction, and adventure. With a career spanning several decades, Fox's storytelling prowess is most evident in his work within the sword and sorcery genre, where he crafted immersive and imaginative worlds. Fox is perhaps best known for his fantasy novels, including Sword of the Seven Suns, which exemplify his talent for blending mythical quests with epic battles and magical elements. His writing is characterized by its vivid world-building, intricate plots, and dynamic characters, reflecting his deep understanding of fantasy lore and adventure storytelling. In addition to his fantasy work, Fox made significant contributions to the comic book industry, creating or co-creating numerous iconic superheroes and characters. His influence extended to science fiction as well, where his innovative ideas and engaging narratives earned him a lasting place in the genre. Fox's extensive body of work showcases his versatility and creativity, leaving a lasting impact on both literary and comic book communities. His ability to weave rich, imaginative stories has solidified his legacy as a master of genre fiction.

CONTENTS

**For unremembered eons the Thing had slept. For
a million years it had quested through the star
worlds of its dreams, until it lived only as a
faint legend in the race memories of mankind. But
now the time had come for man to recall its name,
and to worship it once again. Noorlythin arose
and went out into the world of men and robots.**

The McCanahan came awake in the pearl mists of a Senn dawn, staring upward into the round blue muzzle of a Thorn blaster. The handgun hung in the air without visible support, its trigger moving slowly back. In an instant, it would lash out at him with a thousand tares of destruction.

He whipped the bedclothes into a geyser of silk and moonylon, and dove naked over the edge of the bed to roll on the floor and turn over and over. He brought up against the chair where his uniform belt hung, and fumbled blindly for his service holster.

The blaster spoke in a soft whooosh of yellow flame, and the bedclothes puffed once, billowing into a thick, reddish smoke. *That would have been me, instead of the blankets, if the Little People had not come in my dreams to whisper in my ears of Flaith's loveliness,* the McCanahan thought, and tore loose his addy-gun.

His wrist steadied, and he touched the stud. The blaster, hung on a tensor beam, went red, then white, and began to melt in droplets all over the thick Morrvan carpet of his officer's quarters. The tensor beam, held by a minute mechanism inbuilt within the handgun's butt, let loose, and the blistered, melting thing thudded to the floor.

"It was a close thing," Kael McCanahan told himself, sitting there naked on the floor.

It had been the sfarri who had sent the gun. The sfarri, who hated the men of Terra with a hate like a fierce, blazing flame, who would not scruple at assassination to gain their aims.

They were a cold, efficient breed of men, these sfarri. The farflung Galactic fleet ships of Mother Terra, stretched in a thin line between the stars, had crossed addy beams and searirays with their slim vessels a thousand times. Almost always, Terra lost her ships. Almost always, those far-ranging sfarran ships smashed the eagle-blazoned Terran cruisers, and fled like laughing ghosts into the black infinity of space.

No Terran ship had ever captured a living sfarran. Somehow, with the barbaric philosophy of hara-kari, they committed suicide. It never failed.

And slowly, but remorselessly, the ships of Terra and the Solar Combine were pushed back and back, away from the Rim planets and the close vastness of the Sack worlds that were so rich in every mineral, jewel and foodstuff known to man, and even in some that Terran man had never known.

The Solar Command had ordered Kael's father, Sire Patric McCanahan, Fleet Admiral, with Captain Raoul Edmunds and Commodore Kael McCanahan, to Senorech, there to make at last parlay with the High Mor who ruled the Senn. They were to offer alliances and trade agreements.

Too many times, at the foot of the great ruboid throne of the Senn ruler, had young Kael McCanahan seen the thin, hard lips of the High Mor twist cruelly as he lashed out at the gray-haired Admiral. Too many times had the red flush of fury crept up past his tight white uniform collar with its crimson Commodore braid encrusted thick on its rich surface, as he listened to the High Mor explaining to his father the fact that the men of the Solar Command were no match for the relentless fury of the sfarri.

The High Mor, it was plain, was eager to ally himself with the sfarri.

In return, the sfarri would rid him of these annoying Terrans.

The Thorn blaster that lay melting on the thick pile of his officer's quarters was the opening shot in the extermination program.

The McCanahan let the breath from his lungs in a sudden relief. He sat with his back propped against the leg of the chair, and the hand that held his own Thorn shook so that he put his wrist on his naked knee. He was a tall man, a man grown hard and fit with the mechanical fitness that was the hallmark of all officers of the Solar Intergalactic Command. Blond hair was cropped close to the conformations of his head, giving his face a hard, carven look.

The mark of deep space was in Kael McCanahan's eyes, and in the catlike walk and movements of his big body. He had been processed as only Spacefleet officers were processed, in these days of the Empire, with a cold precision to his mind and a careful hardness to his body.

He came off the floor and began to dress, sliding into the white uniform with its crimson facings, pushing feet into highly polished jet boots. His mind went to his father, the Sire Patric McCanahan, who was Earth representative at the court of the High Mor, overlord of Senorech.

"If they've made their try for me, they've already made it for him," he told the room.

He buttoned his white jacket that had the golden eagles at collar and cuffs. He whipped the leather service belt around his middle. He fastened the black blaster holster to its pivot.

The door opened to a fingerpress, and he was out in the long, metaloid hall, moving with long strides. A woman came out of the shadows to meet him, running.

"Kael! Kael—wait!"

It was Cassy Garson, in her white nursing uniform that was always a little too tight for her curved body. Like many other Earth officers on the distant planets of the empire, the McCanahan had fond memories of the Nursing Auxiliary of the Fleet. Cassy Garson had been a lot of fun, on a dance floor or under the curved canopy of a canalboat, or on the silken cushions of a reflexifloor.

Her soft hands caught his, and he could feel her body's tremblings as she came against him. "Kael, you've heard! Oh, Kael, I'm scared! What'll they do to us?"

"Talk sense, Cassy!" he snapped, knowing his nerves frayed and jumpy because of the metal thing he had melted in his room. He softened his voice, and told her of it.

Her dark eyes were frightened things. "They killed your father tonight! The same way, probably. A Thorn blaster was found a foot from his gloved hand. It looks like suicide. The High Mor has sent word that we're to leave. All of us. No more Earthers on Senorech!"

Cassy whispered in the stillness of the corridor, "We've orders to be aboard the *Eclipse* by noon. To chart our course for Antares. To get out of the Rim planets and stay out."

The McCanahan drew a deep breath. His tight collar choked him, and a vein swelled and throbbed in his hard face. "He's afraid of the sfarri. Sfar is close to the High Mor's home galaxy. May the gods curse a man so driven by fear he'd murder a man who wished him nothing but good!"

Cassy shook against him. "Kael, let's rouse the others! We've got to be on the *Eclipse* by noon!"

There was nothing he could do now, nothing except swallow the bitter truth that he was running from a fight, that he was leaving his dead father on an alien planet with not even a shamrock to blow in the breeze above his grave. His father, one of the Bloody McCanahans, who had scratched their names on graves from Mars to Makron, who had been born to the service of the golden eagles, and now lay with no man to whisper a prayer over his dead body.

McCanahan shook himself like a cat stretching after a sleep. The anger boiled within him, locked inside his guts by his tight lips. "I'm going to get his body, Cassy. I'll take it back with us for decent burial."

Her hands tightened until the red nails cut into his flesh. "You're a fool, Kael McCanahan! A stubborn fool that's walking to his death! Don't you understand? That's just what the High Mor wants you to do! He'll have his dragon killers waiting for you, like cats standing at a mouse-hole in the kitchen flooring!"

"Let them wait," he growled, but her hand dragged him along the corridor, to door after door of the fleet barracks. They roused the honor guard, eighty men in all, the most allowed on Senorech by the High Mor. Men tumbled from their bunks with sleep glazing their eyes, but they wakened fast enough, with Cassy and the McCanahan to whip them into action.

They found Captain Edmunds of the *Eclipse* half dressed. A small, chunky man, he showed the years of his service in the crowsfeet at the corners of his eyes and the faint silver that threaded his curly black hair.

"I'm sorry, Kael. You're The McCanahan now, but that doesn't mean a thing, not after what's happened. Get aboard the ship. I'll bring the men, and whatever they want to take along."

Cassy said, "I've alerted the nurses. They'll be ready at blast-off time."

Within an hour, it was done. Sober men in white uniforms were filing out of their quarters by twos and threes, with their warbags slung over shoulders or hanging by leather thongs from their wrists. They moved across the city in a body, nurses in their center, their hands wrapped on the walnut butts of their service blasters.

McCanahan lost himself five minutes before Captain Edmunds took them out of barracks, toward the silver bullet that was the S.I.C. *Eclipse*. He stepped from Cassy Garson's side, into an intersecting corridor, and moved down a flight of steps to the basement. It was easy, down here among the great heating tubes and dynamos, to stand and wait until the bootfalls faded. Cassy came once to a ramp, and called, but her voice echoed hollowly in the cellar unanswered.

Twenty minutes after they were gone across the city, McCanahan was sliding through the shadows cast by the monolithic buildings, and moving along the broad avenue flanking the Jaddarak canal. Ahead of him were the white bulks of the government buildings. Somewhere in those towering multi-windowed edifices, his father lay dead, with a Thorn blaster close to his hand.

He reached the high stone wall of the gardens and was hoisting himself over the red and stone walltop when a dark-faced Senn caught sight of his Earther uniform and screeched the alarm. The McCanahan cursed in his throat and dropped to the ground inside the garden, his jet boots printing their soles deep in the soft loam of a bed of Thallan sunflowers.

He made for the arched doorway at the near end of the gardens. At a run he came into the darkness of the groined arches. He knew his way through these labyrinthine tunnels. With his father, he liked to walk in the cool corridors where the manacled takkaprots screeched their birdlike songs and the colored waters of the fountains made a rainbow of moving brilliance.

The hoarse, brazen pitch of the bry-horns were startling in the Senorech morning. *They'll be roaming these halls with their blasters cutting at every shadow,* he thought. *Sooner or later one of the shadows they shoot at will be mine!* He had to reach his father's suite, had to kneel there and do what must be done for Patric McCanahan, as Patric had done to his own father before him.

They might expect him to come as he was, expect him to fight his way to his father's side and kneel to whisper a prayer for him over his dead body. On Earth it would be expected. Expected and guarded against. But Senorech was not Earth, and on Senorech things were rarely done for emotional reasons. The McCanahan yanked his Thorn from its sheath as he slid into a telepetor and twirled a dial. If they were expecting him he was ready.

Curiously, the suite of rooms was empty, save for the crumpled man who lay in a white uniform with gold and platinum aigrettes on the shoulders, and red tykkan braid looped under a crumpled arm. McCanahan went to his knees, and his lips moved. In the custom of spacemen everywhere, from the domed tunnels of the Moon to the hellcraters of humid Brinth, he put his hand to his father's wrist and whispered, "I swear by the blood that bonds us, you will not have died in vain. I will make the report, and investigate the reason for your dying."

It was a simple thing, that oath. Many men had spoken it, until it had become a part of the creed of those who roamed the star world. It prevented tragedies, and saved lives, for once the reason for a man's death was known, preventive precautions were taken, so that many men who otherwise would have died, lived to walk the palm terraces of Mars and sail the tossing seas of Achernar. The histories of space featured and explained it, and glamorized its usefulness.

But as the McCanahan let the words trail from his lips, he cursed and looked down at his palm, where part of his father's wrist had come off, to stick to it.

He grimaced, and then reason came into his head. His father was recently dead, no rotting corpse. "Plastiskin," he breathed, and leaned down, ripping with strong fingers at that wrist, carefully built up to hide something.

Around his father's wrist was wrapped a length of silvery wire, thin and fine. The McCanahan leaned forward and untwisted it.

It came away and danced in his fingers, reflecting the blue glow of the wall mercuri-lamps.

"A harpstring!"

He sat on his ankles and forgot that a mile away the *Eclipse* was warming its take-off tubes. "Now why in the name of Brian Born did father hide such a thing on his wrist? He played no harp, nor anything else that ever made music!"

But this was no time to solve puzzles. With a snap of his fingers, he rolled up the silvery wire and bound it tight about an ankle, then thrust his foot back into his service boot. He went to the window and stared down at the splashing fountains and the sunflower gardens half a mile below him. The walls were lined with Senn guards, inside and out, and men with the High Mor's red dragon insignia on their cloaks moved here and there in the shrubbery, slashing at ferns and jungle vines with their swords.

"They'll tire of that soon enough," he decided. "Then they'll come through the palace itself, a floor at a time, working the place over with the point of a dagger and the muzzle of a Thorn."

They would be expecting him to hide. They would be expecting him to keep retreating ahead of them until they trapped him high above, in a cloud-room or on a rooftop. A Senn or a sfarran would act like that. They would do the smart, the sensible thing.

"Faith, my belly tells me it's the smart thing for myself as well," the McCanahan muttered. "But my head tells me something else again."

He wandered the rooms of the palace until he found the wallgrille of an atmosphere tube. With the edge of his service knife, he worked at the screws until the plate came loose from the wall. He crawled into the tube and replaced the grate as best he could. Then, sliding and levering himself from curve to curve of the tube, he began moving downwards.

When he came to gentle loops in the tubes, he let go and slid. It took him three hours to get down, but when he came into the cold metal coils that could duplicate the atmosphere of fifty planets, he was below the search level, and as good as a free man walking the streets.

"Except for the uniform," he told himself, glancing down ruefully at the white and gold resplendence of his fleet garb.

In ten minutes he was crawling up through a street grille, and heading for the space docks.

He was moving up the Avenue of Emblems, with the gleaming bullet that was the S.I.C. *Eclipse* towering above the buildings, nosing its point skyward, still half a mile ahead of him, when he heard the announcers. The words were just sounds, at first, like the pennons flapping above his head from the tall poles, each a gift of the United Worlds.

His mind was torn cleanly with a thin, hard grief, for he was remembering his father, and the way of his smiling and his gentle voice, and the fun they had shared together on the Klisskahaenay Rapids in a boat, or in the crisp darkness of space, with the stars beckoning and his father pointing them out to him. And his handclasp when he left for the Academy, his letters, his visits at holidays when the needs of the Empire were relaxed enough to free the Admiral from his cruiser. It was a good companionship, that of his father and himself, born of their mutual need when his mother died on Aldebaran.

And now it was over. No more would he see that smile or listen to that voice or wonder how it was that his father knew so much more than he about so many things. They would never hook a lyskansa-fish or blast a Martian boar with needleguns. They would never find new foods in restaurants that—

"—under penalty of the red dragon! Repeating! Space Commodore McCanahan—Kael McCanahan, Earther—is to die on sight. All guards are hereby warned. McCanahan must not leave Akkalan. He is to be shot on sight, under penalty of the red dragon! Repeating...."

It sank in after a while. He drew back into the shadows, and the harpstring tied to his ankle pained him, as if it whispered with his father's voice. *They're afraid of me and what I can do to them,* his mind told him. *They don't even dare let me get close to a spacommunicator panel!* But why? Why? The McCanahan shook his head and looked down at himself, neat and trim in the gold and white space uniform.

"It's a card with my name on it asking that they shoot me," he told the shadows. *"I've got to be rid of it or swallow a dozen blaster-beams."*

They would be searching the space docks just about now, minutes before take-off time. They would almost dismantle the ship to find him. And there would be others, blasters in their hands, stretched all around the field. They would shoot on sight, to kill, or they would suffer the fate of the red dragon; and no one in his right mind cared even to think about that punishment, that took a man a month of agony to die.

McCanahan stripped naked in the shadows and bundled his uniform into a ball and weighed it with his boots. He made a compact bundle and threw it up, through the lengthening shadows, onto a low, sloping roof. Let them find that when they could! Then he turned and ran on the sun-warmed bricks, away from the field, toward the dirty alleyways that were the Akkalan slums.

"Now where in the name of the family leprechaun could a man who is stripped to his buff hope to find a shelter in this unholy town?" he asked the wind as he ran.

McCanahan thought of Ars Maasen, a little dark man with a colossal thirst for the pale yellow fire that was Senn wine. His lips twitched as his memory ran on the nights they had spent together in the low-land taverns, sampling every liquid that the skills and arts of men could brew. Ars Maasen traded in lyss furs, and spent his profits faster than the fierce little desert tycats could breed and run to his traps.

With Ars Maasen he would find Flaith.

CHAPTER II

The cities of the Senorech had been built half a million years ago when their primates first modelled clay from mud and water. As the years piled knowledge on their shoulders, their buildings grew and expanded, but they still showed the heterogeneous planning the first Senn had put into them. A man could lose himself in the slum quarter, where the dragon police rarely came, for the High Mor was content to close his eyes to the manner of a man's profit, providing he paid a good tax at the end of the year. Under the creaking signs and iron grille balconies, in the dark street shadows, even a naked man could run free and unmolested.

He came to a square of light and an open door under a carven tycat. Carefully he crept closer listening to the song a hundred throats were bellowing through the smoke and the wine fumes. He came inside on soundless feet and stood sheltered by a solid oak railing.

Flaith was a breath in a man's throat and a catch at his guts, lovely in bronze moire, her amber shoulders bared to the curve of her breasts, the moire slashed teasingly down a naked side to the swell of a white hip. She leaned on the wooden tabletop, and her slant eyes were clear, and her crimson hair a flame caught in the blaze of a wall torch.

The McCanahan let his eyes linger on her loveliness, but it was the little dark man, with the scar across half his face and a full foaming tankard at his mouth, that he had come to see.

He drew back his arm and threw the pebble he held.

Ars Maasen felt the sting of the rock on his forehead. He lowered his mug and swore by a dozen gods at the ill manners of men who would toss rocks in the middle of such a song. And then he felt Flaith's white fingers, and the dig of her long red nails in his forearm.

"It's Kael!" she whispered. "He's naked and alone!"

"For shame! A fine boy like that and—"

"Hssst, you byblow fool!" she warned. "Go to him and see what he needs!"

She pressed the key to her dressing room into his hand, and when he had slipped through the men and women toward the door, she stood so the others could see her. On tiny golden feet she climbed from chair to tabletop, and her bare arms were amber serpents writhing in the crimson half-light.

"The Snakes of Slaamsheel," she called to the players, and a roar of delight went up, for this was an old ballad, and the flame-like Flaith dancing with skirt to mid-thighs across the tabletops, set the blood bubbling in a man's veins.

The McCanahan caught the fire of her throaty singing just as Ars Maasen whipped the cloak off his shoulders and flung it about his chest.

"A full belly, is it?" the dark little man asked. "Wine or Puban ale or maybe both?"

"I'm sober as the snakes Flaith sings of, and as mean!"

Ars Maasen caught the madness in his voice, and grunted, "Come quickly, then. This way, across the sill and through the alley to her doorway!"

When they were moving into the shadows of the alley, Kael told him of his father's death, and of the orders of the High Mor that made him lower than a Tuuran-peddler. And as the words came through his teeth, the raw fury that twisted him showed in his eyes. "They blasted him without a chance for a fight—the way they tried to blast me! Now they're hunting me for a reason only the Shee fairies could know!"

"Easy, boy. Easy! Talk as you want—it helps ease the pain under your navel. But don't let the hate shake you so. It blinds a man."

The little trader turned the key in the lock and the stout wooden door opened inward to a tiny room where an oil lamp cast a dim yellow glare on a dressing table and stool. Costumes hung from a peg-rack on the wall above a tycat-skin couch.

"Flaith's room," he muttered. "Only she comes here."

The McCanahan sat on the couch, and with elbows on knees he looked at the floor and began to swear. He cursed in low Martian, and in fluent English, in high Centauran and sibilant Antaranese. "May the foul fiends of Mars' ten hells gnaw his belly! May the imps of Iseen claw his eyes from now 'til Doomsday! If only Hobgob himself were alive, and here to fly away over Cureeng with his mean little soul!"

Ars Maasen chuckled, and Kael McCanahan bit down on his tongue and glared hard at him. The little man moved to the dressing table and lifted a golden carafe. He went to pour the fiery liquid it held, then turned to glance at the McCanahan. He shook his head and went across the room and gave him the carafe.

"There are times when a man can't quench a thirst, no matter how much he drinks. Take it all."

Kael tilted the carafe and let the smokey quistl slide into his mouth. After a long while he tossed the carafe aside, and drew air into his lungs. He came to his feet and walked up and down.

"I'll need clothes. Some sort of disguise. I can talk their language well enough. I'll make out until the heat ebbs away and I can come back for him. The High Mor! A god and a priest to a god to these heathen Senn! But he's a man, and man can die, slowly and in great pain, when he's hated!"

Ars shook his head. "Go away, yes. But forget this vengeance for a long time. Maybe forever. You'll live longer that way."

Kael put out his hand and lifted the dark man off the floor and shook him. "He murdered my father! Burned him while he slept, with a Thorn blaster on a tensor beam! No way to strike back! No chance to fight for the life he loved!"

He put the little man down and patted his arm. Ars rubbed his chest where his jerkin had pinched his flesh. "You're a strong man, Kael McCanahan. But not strong enough to buck the High Mor on Senorech! I tell you—"

The door came open and Flaith slid in, away from the reek of winey air and the sound of roaring voices. She closed and locked the door and set her back to it.

She was a woman to stir the pulse of a man, in her bronze gown with its slits and deep neck, and the tight fit of its cloth to the swell of her haunches. Her slant eyes with the long curving lashes, the red fullness of a moist mouth and the smooth forehead low under the flaming hair had made her the darling of the quarter. She looked at Kael with her anger bright in her green eyes, and her lips thinned to a tense line.

"Before you speak, Flaith," said Ars Maasen suddenly, "let me tell you he isn't drunk, except with hate for the men that killed his father."

When Ars was done with the story she was in front of Kael whispering softly, "Kael, forgive me! A woman can be a fool! I was one just now, with the thoughts I had of you."

"It doesn't matter. Nothing matters any more except the man I'm going to kill some day! They won't let me leave on the *Eclipse*. They're going to keep me here and hunt me down. And I don't know why!"

Flaith whirled and went to her dressing table. She fumbled at a jar, lifting the lid and dipping her fingers into jet cream. She said, "I'll change the look of your face, Kael honey. Wipe away its hardness and its pain. And somewhere here in all these clothes will be something to fit you. Ars, look among them!"

For an hour the McCanahan sat while they worked on him, and when the hour was done, he stared at himself in the mirror and swore by the eye of Balor himself that no man on all Senorech would know him.

"You're as big and as strong," Ars grinned, studying him. "But you look like a traveling singer, with those short curls and the shadows under your eyes. A man who sings to a woman and loves her, and runs with the dawn!"

Kael snorted, but Flaith nodded.

"A singer or a player of music. Can you use those fingers to coax a tune from anything but a pretty girl?"

Kael laughed. "And what would a man whose family came from Galway be playing? I remember a night I sang of love to a woman on a balcony over the canals of Shar Lir before I put the harp aside and coaxed music from her flesh."

Flaith flushed and scowled, then bubbled laughter.

"You used a harp, that night, you faithless rheenog! A harp that I bought and put aside with my tears, like a moonstruck schoolgirl!"

She fumbled in a chest and drew it out. The lamplight caught its thirty strings and made them glitter. Her fingers stroked it, and her eyes were tender as she lifted them to his face.

Flaith shrugged her shoulders. "I'm crazy. I'm moonstruck and as mad as the ghouls that haunt the rim of Braloom! But—I'm going with you!"

And when Kael would have argued, she put her fingers across his lips and shoved him toward the door.

"Wait outside! Neither you nor Ars nor any man we meet will know Flaith for the shameless little gypsy she's going to turn into! Do you think I want those fingers coaxing music from that harp for anybody but me?"

CHAPTER III

The old rock road from Akkalan to the cities of the Inland Seas is long and broken. Deserts spin their sandy webs across the shards of its ancient cobblestones. Gaunt black ruins of forgotten cities can be glimpsed dimly in the fading sunset, at the foot of the Samarinthine Hills, or standing atop the stone slabs that mark the caravan routes from Pint to Kanadar. Few used the old stone road, and the few who did travel it were so wrapped in their own cares—for this was a road much frequented by criminals and their like—they had no thought for the man and woman who sat by the edge of a running stream, twenty feet from the crumbled side of the highway.

Kael's long fingers swept the taut strings of the silver harp, and a burst of clear sound came flowing forth in a wild, free call. And then the sound was softening, deepening, and in it was something of the peat bogs of Iar Connacht, and something of the chill wind that sweeps the Finnihy from Kenmare to Killarney. A soul wept bitterly in the strings' twanging, with the tears of Deirdre staining its cheeks, and the terrors of Strongbow's son clutching its middle.

"Ai, to be like Ossian, with the power to move men to laughter or to tears with the playing of his fingers on the strings," he whispered to Flaith, where she lay with her chin pillowed on a white fist, staring at him. "But a man does what he can with what he must, and I'm not one for blaming the tool in my hand. It's a good harp."

"It was made by Brith Tsinan," Flaith told him dryly.

The McCanahan opened his eyes at that, and held the harp so as to admire its fluted curve and ornate column. He touched the strings again and they wept at the deftness of his touch. He moved them again and made them laugh.

Flaith wriggled her naked toes to the lilting rhythms he drew from the strings. Across the star lanes and the paths of distant planets, men and women had carried these tunes, and though they lay as dust in their graves, something of their memories sat in Kael McCanahan's fingers this day.

He made the harp sing of Tara and the great hall of Cormac MacAirt, of the baying hounds that ran in the hunts at Clonmell, and the cursing stones of Monasteraden.

The girl rolled on her back in the grass, and the worn cloth of her blouse grew taut across her breasts. "Teach me words to put to those songs, Kael McCanahan," she whispered, "and we'll eat well from the coppers and silver bits we take in the marts like Clonn Fell and Mishordeen."

"Words? Songs? I don't know anything about those. Make up your own words while I play to your ears and the sunlight, and the joy of being alive!"

And at the thought of life, he thought of death, and remembered his father lying on the floor with a Thorn blaster close at hand, and remembered Captain Edmunds and Cassy Garson and the rest who had lifted from Senn in the S.I.C. *Eclipse*, and what had happened to them after that!

He stood suddenly. The scowl was black across his face as he lifted the harp. He threw it from him roughly. Its strings screamed angrily as it skidded across the ground.

"I sit here and play music, and my father calls to me in whatever grave they gave him! I ought to be thinking of finding the High Mor and choking the life from his throat with these hands!"

Flaith put her long fingers to her red hair and shook it free to the breeze. Her slant eyes brooded at him as she remembered that day—weeks back— when they had stood outside the walls of Akkalan watching the destruction of the *Eclipse* under the cruiser beams of the High Mor's space fleet.

Kael had watched, sick and twisted. "That rotten mother's son ordered her smashed! He couldn't find me, so he played it safe and killed them all!"

He went mad for a little while, and Flaith clung to him with sharp nails digging into his arm and back, screaming in his ear. Only when she buried her teeth in his neck and tasted blood did he come back to sanity.

Now, remembering all that, and knowing how the death of his father and the destruction of the *Eclipse* ate in his middle with a sort of sharp, acid bitterness, Flaith watched the McCanahan lift the harp from where he had flung it. A silvern string was curled up, snapped by the rocks across which it had skidded.

"Now, how can we replace that?" Kael wondered. And then his fingers were slipping off his boot and lifting loose the harpstring he had taken from his dead father's wrist.

"It isn't a d-note," he told Flaith, "but it will have to do. I'll not touch it oftener than I must."

He attached the string, and tested it with sweeping fingers. He growled, "Only Ossian himself would know the difference."

The McCanahan brooded less and less in the days that followed, and as they moved along the road that bent in a wide arc about Drekkora and beyond the snowtopped hills of Sharn, he slipped back into the Kael McCanahan she had known in the taverns. Laughter came back to his lips, and he turned more and more to the harp, coaxing magic from its strings, that seemed to soothe his spirit.

As he played, Flaith hummed with him, and words came to her lips, words that matched the wild, clear music, and she sang these words to the ancient melodies, and at last they came to Clonn Fell.

The stalls that lined the Square of the Balang were hung with priceless tapestries from the looms of Beinoll and Drithdraga, and were bright with the potteries of Lamanneen. Men and women of city house and desert tent brushed through the stalls, fingering the wares, haggling over prices, dipping into leather purses for stored coins. Many there were whose fingers waved to the sounds that came from the big fountain in the square where a tall man sat and played a silver harp.

No man would have known the McCanahan in this brown stranger with the naked chest gleaming through the rents of his worn, dusty jerkin, with his loose cloth trousers fastened at naked ankles with metallic cording. And no man would have known Flaith in the dark-skinned gypsy wanton, with her midriff bare above her flapping skirt of transparent teel and below the woven halter that bound her breasts. She was a gamin who laughed and swayed her hips as she sang, and her eyes flashed and flirted with the slack-jawed farmers in from fields and furrows.

A sudden jostling took the farmers and the merchants as they listened to the harpstrings. They made way sullenly for the file of sfarran warriors who came shouldering a path arrogantly through the press. They were tall, handsome men, their lean faces swart and dark. They looked like fighting men, trim in black and gilt field uniforms. Their black eyes moved everywhere, missing nothing.

Now the sfarran detail was closer to the marble fountain where Kael sat with Flaith huddled close against him. He could feel the shiver run through her bare arm where it pressed his side.

She whispered, "They look for us," and her dark eyes surveyed him, studying his disguise. He could read the approval in them.

The sfarri glanced at them and passed on.

A man cursed softly from the shadows. There was a wild flurry of capes and sandalled feet. A peddler, with a scraggly gray beard flowing across his chest, ran like a frightened rat from a group of Kash cattlemen and into a thick thong of rug merchants from Stig.

"A rykinthus peddler," whispered Flaith.

Kael felt the fury rise in him. The sfarri governed the people of this planet as they might a herd of cattle. There was no emotion in the chase. It was hunt and man down, capture him! Take him to the sfarri tribunal, where an atomic disintor ray would blast him into thick white powder.

The peddler ran past Kael on shaking legs.

In his darkest eyes Kael read the angry terror that lay deep within him. Teeth gritted, Kael moved clumsily, bumping into the foremost of the sfarri pursuers, throwing him off balance. Two others ran into him and fell heavily to the cobblestones of the square.

The sfarran officer rose, tight-lipped at this clumsiness. His hand went to the holster of his addy-gun. Kael rammed a fist to his middle and slid sideways, his harp still in his hand. With a backward lash of his arm he drove the harp's heavy crown into his temple.

The blow knocked the harp from his hand. He scrambled after it, where it lay on the cobblestones. His fingers missed as he snatched at it and swept across the strings. At the harsh, discordant sound that rose into the air the sfarran officer who had been reaching for him fell awkwardly to the stones, sprawling lifelessly.

Other sfarri were falling too, as if the breath of life had been blown from them. They lay here and there beside the fountain, like dead men.

Kael stared dumbly, hearing the shouts of the people of Clonn Fell falling back from the lifeless sfarri.

Then he whirled and slipped in among the crowding merchants and farmers, pretending that he was driven by stark terror.

A moment of wild, flurried movement, and he was free, darting behind a wooden wagon toward the heavy drapes of a carpet stall. Flaith was shrinking back, also losing herself in the milling mob.

Kael saw her, dove toward her.

She cried out, "What was it? How'd you do it? What killed them?"

"I don't know! We have no time to play guessing games!"

He caught her hand, dragged her into an alleyway where the massive stone walls of ancient buildings towered high above them. The dark shadows they cast lay like shielding hands that shrouded them in sudden darkness.

Flaith panted, "You touched your harp! It made a sound! That must have done it!"

"I know all that! But for the sake of your unborn children, stop talking and run!"

They went swiftly through the narrow streets, burdened only by the silver harp. Under a stone archway, Kael swung to the right. A small figure stood in the doorway, beckoning to them. It was the bearded peddler Kael had saved from the sfarri.

"This way," the peddler called. "Lunol forgets no man who saves him from death!"

An oak door opened. From it, a stone stair led down into a pit of Stygian blackness. The peddler put a hand on Kael's belt, dragging him down into the gloom. They went swiftly, toward a stream of water that rushed and gurgled darkly between two narrow paths of brick that jutted outward from the sheer rock walls.

"The sewer system of Clonn Fell! Quickly, along the ledge! Gods be with us! If the sfarri follow and clap their hands on us they'll throw us to their torturers!"

The peddler whimpered in his fear as he scurried along the narrow brick ledge. Kael and Flaith ran after him. Soon their sandals were wet with the accumulated filth and slime of centuries. They moved swiftly, with the dim light of tiny bulbs, high in the domed ceiling, guiding their feet.

They went for miles through the sewer, deep down under the streets of Clonn Fell.

When they emerged into bright sunlight, they stood on a wide beach where the gray, cold waters of the Taganian Sea rolled restlessly.

Flaith sank on a rock, one hand pushing back her thick red hair. Kael read her weariness in her haggard face.

"Why were the sfarri after you?" he asked the peddler. "What did you do?"

Lunol shrugged. "I dwell in the Clith Korakam desert that stretches from the ocean here to the cliffs of Kamm."

Kael frowned his puzzlement.

It was Flaith who explained. "The black tower of Balzel lies in the Clith Korakam desert. It is a place forbidden to all people of Senorech."

The old man whimpered his fright. "I saw a man come out of that tower. It was many months ago. He was a tall man with a bald head and scrawny, withered arms. And yet there was something in the manner of his walking, something in the way he held his head, that sent a cold chill of terror down my spine!

"Since then I have had dreams. Terrible, frightening dreams! Dreams of places where no man has ever been! The sfarri have been hunting me since then. It took them a long time to find me, but now—"

Lunol shrugged. "From here it is not far to Clith Korakam. Once I am on its sands no man will ever be able to find me! I've spent all my life on those sands. I know them as I know the fingers of my hands."

Kael looked at Flaith. "Sure, they'll be after us, too, now! They know what we look like. They'll want us for helping this one get away."

"What can we do?"

The old peddler smiled. His swart face lighted under the loose cowl of his kufiyah.

"Come with me. I will make a home for you on the desert where none shall ever find you."

Flaith said, "Perhaps they won't know about us. We left the sfarri lying like dead men, remember!"

Lunol looked his interest.

Kael said, "I touched my harp and the sfarri fell like poisoned insects. Why they fell I do not know. Do you?"

Lunol shrugged his shoulders. "I am an ignorant man. I do not know about these things. But this I do know. If we do not go into the desert, sooner or later the sfarri will find us!"

They set off across the sands, past the high-humped rocks that were beaten and weathered by the fierce storms that ravaged the planet. They struggled across the burning wasteland, their throats choked with the heat and the sand.

The sun glowed down on them, making sweat run in tiny rivers that plastered their robes to their flesh. The hours went by. Night came, and they slept where they fell, exhausted.

With the sun, they were up and moving. The days came and went, long eternities of heat and thirst, through which they plodded in the shifting sands. They were tiny motes of life against a backdrop of level, desolate loneliness.

They crossed ancient beds of rock, where once, in forgotten eons, a sea had rolled. Here Kael had to lift and carry Flaith, for her thin sandals were gone, and her white feet were red with blood where the stones had cut them.

They went on and on. They stopped at an oasis, here and there, to quench their thirst in the cool waters of a subterranean spring. They ate of the dried figs and bits of hard black bread that Lunol carried in his girdle.

Toward dusk of their sixth day on the desert, Lunol cried out. They focussed eyes salt-encrusted with dried sweat where his finger pointed.

"There! See yonder, and know Lunol did not lie!"

There was livid fear in the eyes of the old peddler as he gestured at the glistening black pile of the tower lifting upward from the sand. It was almost as if he expected to see something dark and fearsome slip from the basalt blocks and come hunting him.

"It's been there for thousands of years," he whimpered. "Even when the balangs roamed these sands, the tower was there."

Flaith came close to Kael. "I'm frightened! There's something wrong with it."

Kael snorted and walked forward through the sand, ploughing his way where the wind had piled thick granules. Flaith ran a few steps after him, her hand seeking his arm. Behind them, could hear the peddler moaning.

"I tell you," he chattered, "I've seen it come out of the tower on clear nights when there wasn't a wind stirring across the sand. It just moved around, all white and shining, making the sand lift and whirl, like a storm down off the Barakian hills. It was cold. Terribly cold! The sand was frozen solid where it had been."

The McCanahan stared at the tower. It was tall, formed of black basalt, a thick column of rock that was windowless and seemingly doorless. At the base of the column was a long, low building that stretched on either side of the tower for forty feet. Two red pylons, carved and polished, stood like pointing fingers at its ends.

The old peddler was wringing his hands. "It wasn't human, that thing. It could kill as easy as a harlot winks! Once I saw a hare run past it. It stretched out a thin wire of that cold white stuff and touched the rabbit, and the rabbit died. I'm afraid!"

Kael turned and caught the old peddler, yanking him to him.

"You've bleated and brayed ever since we got out of Clonn Fell! Go back if you want!"

The old man's eyes glazed in his brown face. A wind stirred the wisps of whitish hair that straggled from under his kufiyah, and the springs of thin beard that fluttered on his chin. He seemed to shake himself, and at an effort, his eyes cleared.

"No! No! You saved me from the sfarri. I told you the tower was the only place where the sfarri never came, on all of Senn. But to go to the tower, to meet that thing—"

The McCanahan let the old man go, gently. He was ashamed of the burst of rage that had shaken him. He drew in a lungful of the hot desert air. He was alone on Senn. His comrades in the *Eclipse* had been destroyed. The High Mor was seeking him across a world, and to have this peddler whimpering his fear in his ears was proving too much.

He said gently, "Sorry, old one! Sooner or later the sfarri will come here to the tower. After they have searched all Senn. They will find us. Maybe inside that tower—"

Lunol shivered. "No man can live inside the tower. No man can approach it. Death strikes down all who try! I've seen too many animals run close to it and—hofff!—they go up in smoke! There's a band of death all around it. If you go too close, you'll be the one to turn into smoke!"

Kael McCanahan shrugged. "As well go up in smoke as die under a Thorn blaster held in a sfarran hand!"

He went on alone.

Flaith whimpered, watching him. She crouched, her long-nailed fingers digging into the soft flesh of a white thigh. Her eyes were wide, frightened.

He went twenty feet, then thirty. He grew smaller, walking across the flat stretch of dunes toward the great black tower.

As he walked, the McCanahan threw his blaster, fastened on a length of rope, ahead of him. If some electrical force was probing, it would seek out the metal of his addy-gun and shatter it.

Nothing happened to the gun.

He walked on and on.

No death struck at him. Now he stood under the shadow of the great gateway that was formed of a queer, sleek marble that held green fire frozen beneath its glazed surface. He put a hand on the gate and pushed.

To his surprise, the doorway opened, noiselessly.

Kael moved under the arched gateway, into a region of dim light and sharp black shadow, where a towering pile of glass and metal bulked huge in the center of the hall.

And then his legs crumbled beneath him, and Kael McCanahan went down, onto the tiled yellow flooring of the tower room.

CHAPTER IV

He floated bodiless in space. The stars swirled about him, moving endlessly in their orbits. This was death, he knew. But it was a strange form of death, for here and there he could recognize familiar constellations, saw nebulae and galaxies that he knew.

This is not Noorlythin!

The voice swirled about him, rumbling out of the black stretches of space itself. The McCanahan could feel eyes on him, hidden eyes that probed at him, lancing through him with the remorseless certainty of a surgeon's electroniscalpel.

This is a Terran. A man named McCanahan. He is frightened!

He was within the tower. Only Noorlythin could live in that trap of hell. I do not understand!

Something touched him, as gently as a Spring breeze off the sea. And with the touching, the eyes of Kael McCanahan came open to the robed figures that floated between the stars. He tried to see their faces, but only a blinding whiteness returned his stare, under the low hoods of the robes.

Seek not our faces, Terran. To you, we are as the sun!

His tongue was thick and swollen. He mumbled. He swallowed, as if to clear his throat.

"Where am I? Who are you? I walked into the tower and—"

What had happened to him on that yellow floor? His knees had buckled and he had gone down with an intangible force crushing him. Kael shook his head.

We are the Doyen. An ancient race, a race of once-men who have lived out the span of our lives a million centuries. In that time, we changed. Our bodies evolved upward from their primal shape, striving always to progress to that last, final shape of all.

"Noorlythin? He is one of you?"

Once he was. But Noorlythin could never forget the adoration that was showered on us by the sfarri. He hungered to be worshipped as a god, as once he was, many eons ago. Noorlythin turned his back to us, the Doyen. He has gone back, resuming the primal shapes of the men whose race is young.

Fear came to McCanahan there among the stars. It crept in through the unspoken words of the robed things, clutching at his mind with frozen fingers. He shook uncontrollably before he could assert himself.

"This Noorlythin. You seek him?"

He has broken the Doyen law. He has become as an animal. With his powers, he can be a god to any primal race. No primate can stand to him, and well he knows it. When he is ready, when he has used the sfarri to conquer all the primal races of the galaxy, he will ascend into the living sacristy of the Temple of Sharrador. There, once again, he will be worshipped with living sacrifices, with orgies that only a primal race can conceive and execute.

The McCanahan said, "You aren't telling me all this just to talk."

You are a poor servant. Your flesh is weak. Yet must we use you against Noorlythin!

"How? How can I help?"

And then all space was shaking, flowing in a liquid stream, inward toward a whirlpool of light that swam around and around, sucking the stars and the black deeps of space into its maw. And as the stars and space flowed faster and faster, so flowed McCanahan stretched and lengthened and tortured....

He sat on the yellow tile of the ancient tower. A tumble of red hair shifted and tossed before him as Flaith's white hand shook him. Beyond her, near the open green marble door, stood the peddler. His eyes burned with the fright in his face.

"Kael! You were so still. I thought you dead!"

She helped him to his feet. He swayed, almost retching with the pain that spasmed his muscles. Flaith was a blur of white before him. He put his hands to her soft shoulders, and his fingers dug in. He held to her, as to reality.

Slowly the floor solidified and steadied beneath his buskined feet. The pain slid away, slowly, then with greater speed.

"Out there," he said thickly. "Things. Bright things. Maybe made of energy itself. They spoke to me. Told me about something named Noorlythin. It was as if I was suspended in space itself. Want me to help them."

Flaith came against him until the hard tips of her breasts burned his naked chest. Her voice was a flow of terrified sound.

"The Doyen! They are the Doyen! We on Senn always thought they were just a myth, like the balangs! They are gods, Kael! The gods of all space!"

The McCanahan grunted. "Well, gods or not, they want to make a servant out of me. They want me to help them round up some character named Noorlythin."

From the doorway the peddler groaned. His eyes rolled in his head. A white froth bubbled on his lips.

"Noorlythin, the evil! Noorlythin, who lived in the olden days, when all Senorech worshipped him with blood sacrifices. Even today, on the altar in the Temple of Krebb, the dark stains are still there!"

The McCanahan turned away to stare upward at the great metal machine that bulked monstrous in the dim light. It was formed of black steel and silvery chrome. Its tubes and power relays were inset under thin glass globules so that it resembled a gigantic, transparent-backed spider. High above its arching shell, reaching upward into the dimness of the tower itself, were half a hundred floating, glowing balls that danced and spun in the wind eddies.

Stretching on either side of the central hall were wide corridors, their walls lined by glass bubbles that projected outward like bulging eyes.

The McCanahan moved toward the near corridor, his eyes caught by a scene within one of the glassine bubbles. Flaith followed him, afraid to be alone.

They halted before a curving prism, discovering it to be a dioramic window that seemed to peer into the heart of a distant planet. Flaith whispered, "It's the planet Sfar! I'd know those cold-faced men anywhere!"

Frozen, tiny faces stared back at them from a great, white city, set like a jewel on the shore of a wide, blue sea. The little figures were caught in a locked moment of time, attending to their duties. Some moved with weapons, some drove sleek monocars.

"There's something about them," Kael muttered, scowling. "They're so perfect! They make every move count as if it would be their last. Each of them is long and lean, with bright, keen eyes that never miss a thing!"

Flaith put a hand on the glassine bubble, leaning closer, staring down at the magnified scene. "It's funny, but—"

Her slant eyes slid sideways at the McCanahan, amusement swimming in them. "I've noticed something that I thought *you'd* see, Kael McCanahan!"

His eyes studied the girl in front of him as she cocked her head at him. Even in her tattered garments, through which the McCanahan caught disturbing glimpse of white, rounded flesh, the redhaired Flaith was a tantalizing morsel of womanhood. He put out a long arm and drew her in against him.

"Och, now what would I have been missing that you, with your cat's eyes, have seen?"

She shrugged elaborately. "If you haven't missed them, I won't tell—"

"Shades of Bridget na Gablach! Their women!"

"They have no women! No man of Senorech has ever seen a sfarran girl. Rumor says that they shelter them because of their loveliness. But if this a diorama of the sfarran planet, and there are no women, then—"

Kael grunted. "You and your crazy theories! Look, woman! See for yourself. There are women there. There must be women!"

But though they hunted along all that corridor, staring at the sfarran world and its divers shapes and colors, its desert storms and wind-tossed seas, its magnificent white cities that looked like milky jewels, they found no woman.

For two hours they hunted, until the McCanahan discovered that by moving a red lever he could make the scenes within the bubbles come to life. The tiny men moved, as if released from a frozen tomb. They walked and piloted their vessels, and went about their tasks. Yet even so, no woman appeared.

"It's some sort of televisic communicator," the McCanahan muttered, "that's spacecasting across a billion billion miles of space."

"They have no hospitals, either," said Flaith in a troubled voice.

"Now what will you be meaning by that?"

The redhead smiled wryly. "Even in this advanced day and age on Senorech, Kael my darling, women still go to hospitals to have their babies!"

The McCanahan scowled. "And if there are no hospitals, they'll have their brats at home, won't they?"

"Brats, indeed!" flared Flaith, whirling, chin high.

"Peace, peace," grinned Kael. "It's only teasing I was. But I begin to see your drift, mavourneen. No women, no hospitals, no children. Then the sfarri are not human. Or maybe it's because they're ovopoid. Maybe they're sexless, like an amoeba, or maybe they fertilize themselves and lay an egg to hatch a little sfarran."

"There are no little sfarri. All are grown men. Every last one."

McCanahan brooded with his lower lip thrust out. "No little ones. No coibche to bind a man and a woman in holy matehood. No women, even, to comfort a man when he's sad with loneliness. Then they aren't human, with no heart in their chests to beat a little faster at the kiss from a woman's lips. And if they have no hearts, they must be—

"Robots!"

The McCanahan walked in his excitement, taking long steps that drew him past the metal machine with its glass-encased tubes and wirings. *"Robots!* No wonder they're perfect! No wonder it is that none has ever been caught by a Terran battle fleet for questioning! Being robots, they destroy themselves before capture. And being robots, too, they fight with the same mechanized, incredible fury that's smashed a dozen war fleets between Achernar and Sol."

The McCanahan was warming to his subject. "We fought the sfarri across a score of galaxies, ever since my grandfather Rhoderick—bless his memory!—first crossed atomic disintegration beams with their cruisers. They've pushed us back, away from the Rim planets. Everywhere our paths have met, there's been bloody war. Bloody? Ha! There's been no blood spilled on their side. Just cogs and wheels and wire!"

Flaith tossed back a lock of reddish gold hair from before her eyes. "You killed them in Clonn Fell. You slew them when you touched your harp strings! The sound did it."

"The harp of Brith Tsinan. Aie! It had the silver string that I took from my father's wrist attached to it. Do you remember how I broke the other, when I threw the harp on the road from Akkalan? Where is the harp, Flaith?"

The old peddler came shuffling forward from the doorway, dropping his shoulder to loosen the strap that held the black sack to his back. From the sack the bright silver harp tumbled into the McCanahan's eager fingers.

He lifted the harp and set it to his shoulder. His hands played across the strings, and the wild sharp peal of the strings swept up and through the tower.

In answer to the high, keening notes, a tube in the great metal machine spanged shrilly. The tinkle of broken glass was loud in the sudden silence as Kael dropped his fingers from the quivering harp strings.

Lunol, the peddler, cried out harshly, his face a wet mass of sweating fear. Flaith screamed high and shrill. Her bare arm lifted and pointed.

The McCanahan whirled, and his harp fell from numb fingers.

Bright and blazing, like the core of a giant sun, a whirling mass of fiery matter whirled and quivered, pulsing before the great machine. Its incandescence was blinding, brilliant. They could read the fury in the flame of its sentient heart. They needed no voice to tell them.

Noorlythin!

The sunburst of brilliance lifted, shuddering. It foamed and grew, incandescent in the sheer brilliance of the white fire that burst and bloomed within it.

A thin stream of fire reached out, touched Lunol and laved him in its blinding whiteness.

And Lunol shrank in upon himself, grew smaller, almost tiny within the bubble of brilliance that held him. He grew, then. Expanded suddenly. And where Lunol and the hungry white fire had been was just blackened smoke, drifting across the yellow floor.

Flaith turned her face in against Kael's chest. Her fingers bit their nails convulsively into his flesh. Her body shook so badly that its trembling moved the McCanahan as he stood on firmly planted legs.

Another pencil of fire stabbed out.

Stabbed out, and—

Halted!

In midair it halted, spreading across an invisible wall of nothingness that was erected before the McCanahan and the girl he held.

There was puzzlement in the pulsing of the thing, in the blind, angry dartings of the pencil-beam of flame. It moved to the floor, and quested upward to the ceiling. It darted from wall to wall, seeking to penetrate the barrier that sheltered its victims.

And now the amazement was gone. The white fire burned lower, as if afraid.

In sheer anger, that made it blaze so brightly that Kael cried out and lifted a hand to hide his face, the thing stabbed again. And again, hungrily, raging with insane fury.

The Doyen shelter you! Only the Doyen could stand against the power of my will!

McCanahan could feel the anger fall away before the fear that ate at the thing. Almost, he could hear its thoughts. Perhaps it wanted him to hear his thoughts.

They can save you for a little while. But they cannot shelter you forever. Not from Noorlythin-the-Doyen can they save you forever! I shall work my will on you yet, man of Terra! You will crawl on bloody stumps for legs, waving handless arms for mercy! Begging me with tongueless mouth for the boon of death!

It came to McCanahan that the thing spoke out of the grip of its own, paralysing terror. It mouthed threats to bolster its own esteem.

Kael put his mind to the task and forced a laugh between his lips. He made his laugh mocking, challenging.

"You'll never kill me, Noorlythin! I am servant to the Doyen. Such as the Doyen protect those whom they select to serve them!"

The thing that was Noorlythin pulsated like a stream of cobwebs caught in a mad wind. It lifted and shook, swirled and bellied.

And then, suddenly, it was quiet. It hung a foot above the yellow tile, barely moving. And the inertia of the thing was more frightening than all its blinding brilliance.

The Doyen play the game according to its rules. They will not let me harm you with my Doyen powers. Only by other gifts can I let the life from your body, Terran! So be it!

CHAPTER V

And the thing was gone, blanking instantly from sight with nothing left behind to show its presence but a bit of black dust stirring restlessly on the tiling as a breeze came in off the desert and moved down the long corridor.

"Poor Lunol," whispered Flaith. "Oh, the poor old man!"

The McCanahan lifted his harp and stared dumbly at its glittering surface of polished silver. "The string from my father's wrist broke the tube in the machine. It summoned up Noorlythin from—from wherever he was hidden."

"How can you use that knowledge?" wondered Flaith.

Kael shook his head. "I don't know yet. But I will. Somehow, I'll find out the truth." He lifted his head and peered about the great tower. "And where better to begin than here?"

They ate dried meat plucked from Flaith's girdle-pouch, chewing on hard black bread. And then they slept, with Flaith cuddled against the McCanahan's length, with his own head pillowed on an arm, both of them stretched at the foot of the great metal machine.

It was the McCanahan who stirred first, rising from the soft body of the girl, carefully so as not to disturb her. He wandered about the tower, studying the strange machines that glistened at him from the shadows. A man would need a dozen lifetimes to understand these things, he told himself. He would find no help from them.

He tried to fight the pall of bitter despair that lay across his shoulders. He was the servant of the gods of space, caught up by them to hunt out and punish another god.

Laughter touched his lips; but the bitterness in it stung like acid.

How does one fight a god? How does one go about killing a thing that is made only of white, radiant energy? A thing that by a mere touch of the blazing brightness that comprises it, can blast him and all his kind to a black dust that shifts restlessly across a floor, flung by an errant breeze!

His fists were clenched until the knotted muscles of his forearms ached. "I can't do it," he told the machines. "I'm only a man. I can't fight against a god!"

Deep within him, he knew that someone had to make this fight, that someone from one of the thousands of Terran worlds had to face Noorlythin, had to stand to him and his awesome power, or the human race itself would go down, crushed and torn and flung into nothingness, as a sand castle went down before the relentless roll of the ocean.

When that happened, the sfarri and the Senn would expand, would lift their faery castles and their monstrous, monolithic palaces, where now Terran buildings stood. And those of the Senn would have their pick of the women of Earth.

Of women like—

Flaith!

He turned to find her stretched on her back, her eyes regarding him wistfully. A shred of her gypsy costume was caught over one shoulder, falling away from the push of her nearly bared breasts. The thin stuff at her waist hugged round hips and full upper thighs. The breath caught in the McCanahan's throat as his eyes ran over her.

She was a woman to steal the breath of a man from his lungs, and send his senses running in a saraband. She was the dream of every lonely spaceman at his battle station, of every thul-prospector hanging to a wandering asteroid with fingers and a suction clamp. With her red hair frothing over the witchery of her cream-skinned shoulders, she was Deirdre herself, the perfect woman.

Something of his tangled senses came to Flaith and she laughed, with the throaty womanness of her pleased at the worship in his eyes.

In the middle of her laughter, a shadow came and lay on the yellow flooring between them.

A sfarran officer stood tall and lean in the open doorway of the tower, a glittering Thorn blaster in his right hand.

The officer regarded them coldly. It came to Kael as he stood dumbly returning that hard glance, that he had never seen a sfarran smile.

"You will come with me at once."

He stood sideways to the green marble doors, giving them room to pass him. Flaith scrambled to her feet; eyeing the gesture with which the officer moved his blaster. The McCanahan bent and lifted his harp, and thrust it into the black sack that had once belonged to dead Lunol the peddler.

Then he was walking with Flaith out the pylon gateway of the tower, across the hot sands toward the black hull of a sleek sfarran cruiser.

He was midway through the hatch when he paused, staring.

There were sfarran men and officers inside the ship, but they were slumped over queerly, in distorted postures and attitudes. He had seen the sfarri like that in Clonn Fell, when he had plucked at the strings of his harp. But here he had not struck those strings!

Last night he had played for Flaith and Lunol. And when he had played, a tube in the great, glistening tower machine had cracked into a thousand different fragments.

That breaking tube might have summoned up Noorlythin from whatever hell he dwelt.

"Move in, Earther," said the officer behind him.

Kael went with Flaith, at the officer's orders, to an upholstered bench set against a panelled wall. The officer brooded at them, and they could read the raw hate that lay deep in his black eyes.

The officer said, "You ought to be rayed down here, to save the High Mor the agony of listening to your pleas for mercy. But yours is a grave offense. An offense no man or woman has ever committed before. It calls for grave punishment."

Flaith's hand trembled in Kael's big fist.

The officer said, "The High Mor commissioned me to bring you to him. I would be derelict in my duty were I to do otherwise. And I, Captain Herms Borkus, intend to commit no such infraction."

The black eyes studied them. There was curiosity swimming in their depths, mixed with the hot hate, and a grudging respect. He turned away and went forward to the control chamber. Kael could hear the clicking relays picking up the automatic transmission. The ship lifted easily, its null-gravity humming with smooth insistence.

Flaith whispered, "The harp, Kael. You'll kill him as you killed the others!"

But Kael only gestured at the sfarri that lay in the strange and distorted attitudes, or sprawled on the floor. And even as he gestured, the first of these dead sfarri stirred and sat up, looking about him. Others moved then, silently, turning at once to their duty posts, resuming their tasks as if they had never been interrupted.

"Mother of balangs!" whispered Flaith, her eyes wide and troubled under their long red lashes. "They live!"

The McCanahan was half out of his seat, his mind questing. *They were dead, but now they live. Like machines, turned off and on!* He thought of the cracking tube in the black tower, and the sfarri that had fallen in the square in Clonn Fell. Dimly, he began to grasp the power of the harpstring that he had lifted from his father's wrist. It smashed the tubes in the power-boxes that fed the sfarri their energy. Without that power, they were idle machines.

With the trained mind of the spacefleet officer, he saw the possibilities of such harpstring, in the form of a vibrator that would spacecast a flow of microwaves from the battle wagons of the fleet. With a series of these vibrations fanning out ahead of them, Solar Combine ships could more than hold their own with the sfarri. For at the touch of those microwaves, the sfarri that ran their spaceships would slump in their form of death.

Bitter mockery rose inside the McCanahan as he sat hunched over. He had the knowledge, but what use was it? He was being carried to an extremely painful death in the damp dungeons of the High Mor's palace.

Herms Borkus came toward them from the control chamber. He stared from one to the other. At last he said, "How did you do it? In Clonn Fell, we found our officers and men lying as if dead. As this ship neared the Tower of Noorlythin, my men slumped over unconscious."

Kael shrugged. "I've a powerful evil eye, friend. I cast it at those I don't like and—well, you saw the result."

Borkus said coldly, "You talk foolishly. There is no such thing as the evil eye. What is the answer?"

"Oh, now look!" began Kael, when the thought struck him. *Borkus is a sfarran, yet he did not succumb to the lack of power!* Kael turned the words on his tongue, and said, "I was talking sense, captain. In my family, as far back as the time of Niall of the Nine Hostages himself, one of the McCanahans has always possessed the evil eye. It's a daft thing, and I'm not understanding it myself, any too well, but it's the only explanation I can give."

Borkus looked at Flaith, but his eyes did not linger on her beauty, and showed no more emotion than a dog would show staring at a building. From Flaith, his eyes swung to Kael who could read the thought that was gripping the officer. *He's wondering if he can strike at me through her.* But that was the way of a man who lacked confidence in his own abilities, and Kael knew that this man before him had powers he had not yet used.

The sfarran captain shrugged and moved away. He threw back over his shoulder, "The High Mor will know how to deal with you. After all, it is his duty, not mine."

For five hours, Flaith and McCanahan huddled together on the upholstered bench in the sfarran ship. With each passing moment, the bleakness in the soul of the McCanahan grew darker and more empty.

The ship landed on the palace grounds, shuddering slightly as it dropped onto the metallic tanbark. A moment after its vanes were clamped, Flaith and the McCanahan were crossing the landing field, moving down a stone ramp that led to the dungeons.

A burly man, with black hair matted over his naked chest, clanked a ring of keys at their approach. He preceded them along the torchlit corridor until he paused at an empty cell.

The cell was unlocked, and the McCanahan thrust inside. And then a sobbing Flaith was dragged away from him, in the grip of one of the burly man's hairy paws.

Kael McCanahan was a spaceman, and spacemen are generally, without quite being aware of it, excellent philosophers. He tested the bars of the cell, found them to be formed of Mollystil, and went over to the cot, where he lay on his back, staring at the blank ceiling. Within five minutes he was asleep.

He woke to the touch of a soft hand on his chest, to find a woman bent above him, her limpid brown eyes soft with pity. A tumble of yellow hair framed her oval face.

"I bring you food and drink, lord. You will need your strength for what lies ahead."

Kael laughed harshly. "Better to be weak and near death when the High Mor begins his tortures."

She moved closer. She was fragrant with some Senn perfume, and the little she wore—a red silk thing twisted about her loins, with a slavegirl's golden chains about her throat—showed her body to be exquisite, even in the half-light of the cell. The McCanahan read the pity in her eyes, and began to take interest.

"Sometimes, those live the longest who have no false pride," she told him.

"You give me hope. Were you sent to do that?"

There was reproach in her eyes, and she started to draw away. The McCanahan caught her slim wrist and held her.

"Who sent you with your tempting offers?"

She pouted at him. "No man sent me. I am Slyss, the slave girl from Aakkan." She rubbed her wrist when he released her, unconsciously posing for his eyes.

The McCanahan said, "Tell me more!"

But she shrugged a white shoulder and went to stand by the cell bars while he ate. When he was done, she took his tray and wooden bowl and mug, and walked off with them, unlocking the cell door with a key that hung from her wrist, attached to a thick metal manacle.

Her hips wriggled as she went, and she threw a glance at him over her shoulder. Her voice was music as she carolled a farewell.

She left the McCanahan with a fever of impatience in him. He strode back and forth in his cell. His hands tested the Mollystil bars a hundred times. He told himself that the Senn did not love the sfarri overmuch, that the Senn, being descended from animal ancestors, had no common ground with a race of robot men. He asked himself where in this pile of giant masonry Herms Borkus had hidden Flaith. If he could get away, if he could use this yellow-haired slave girl to unbar these cell doors for him, he would find Flaith and flee.

Flee?

Where on all Senorech was there sanctuary for Kael McCanahan?

The slave girl told him when next she brought his food. This time, he was awake and restless, and her soft, quick tread was like music to his ears.

She came close to him, with only the width of the little tray between his chest and her breasts that stirred gently to her quickened breathing. Her brown eyes were full of gentle pity as they studied his haggard face and sunken eyes.

"Lord, you were never meant for prison bars! If only you would trust me, I know a way that leads from the palace."

"Trust you, Slyss? I'd love you for a chance at freedom."

Again she preened, smiling as he wolfed the food. "Only for that?"

His eyes studied her. She was a lovely thing, slim and gently rounded. Beside the flame-haired Flaith she was a cooling breeze, but he knew many men who would have walked through the fires of Nanakar for an hour in her arms.

"Not only for that," he told her. "You're a sight to send a man's blood to pounding in his veins. You don't look like a slave girl. You're much too beautiful."

Her laughter was soft, pleased. She came and sat beside him, so that her hip and thigh were warm on his. She carried perfume in the yellow hair that dripped on her shoulders. It was rare perfume, and the McCanahan thought that if her mistress knew about it, that creamy back would be striped with red whipwelts.

"There are men of the Senn who hate the sfarri," she whispered close to his ear. "Rumors have come to them that you possess some strange weapon, some magic means of killing the hated sfarri."

The McCanahan swallowed the cheap wine that had been chilled in a coil of refrigerated stil. He nodded. "I know a way."

It was on his lips to say more when his sidewise glance surprised a momentary gleam in the gentle brown eyes. He needed no psychiatrist to read that triumph for him, even though it was quickly veiled behind her curving lashes. *Now why should a slave girl of the palace know that feeling because of what I said?* he asked himself.

The McCanahan put his arm about the girl, drew her in against him. With his lips buried in the yellow mass of her hair, he whispered, "It ought to be worth a lot to the Senn to get that knowledge! With such a weapon they need never fear the sfarri again. They could cast them out! Even seek alliance with the Solar Combine!"

It was his last words that tensed the muscles across her soft back. Instantly, the muscles were relaxed, and she melted closer against him, her soft lips moving across his face to find his lips.

The McCanahan kissed her. Why not? But he was warned, and only a fool disregards a warning. And Kael McCanahan, as he drank from the scented lips of Slyss the slave girl, was even then congratulating himself that no McCanahan was ever a cursed gossoon.

He let her go after a while. She was a pleasant little thing, but she was no Flaith. He said, "Suppose I agree to trade my weapon for freedom from the High Mor? How do I know the Senn can guarantee my liberty?"

"I have the keys," she whispered. "Tonight I will come for you, to lead you through the dungeons, to the vaults below the dungeons, where the sea seeps in through solid rocks. No sfarran ever walks down there. It is a dead, damp place. But the Senn go there to hide from the sfarri. It is the one safe place on all Senorech. Slyss will take you there."

He lingered over her lips, close by the unlocked cell door, to bind their bargain. But when she was gone, he took to pacing his cell, his brows drawn together. She wants more than the body of Kael McCanahan, that one, he told himself. The weapon I possess, and me! Or am I playing the buffoon in thinking she was fond of me? He went back over their meetings and discovered to his chagrin that each of her moves seemed calculated. Like a sfarran! Cold, careful! Even her kisses lacked the fire such a woman should bring to them!

As the sun sank below the hills above Akkalan, the McCanahan rested. He was fresh when Slyss came to him on her bare feet, her key grating silently into the cell lock. "Slib, the jailer, lies drugged with wine," she told him. "He won't stop us."

She went quickly along the cell corridor ahead of him. At an intersection in the rock walls she slipped to the right, into dark shadows. He heard the rough grate of metal, and a section of the floor was rising and falling, as a balanced slab of rock fell back to expose a number of handhewn stone ledges that served as steps.

Slyss went first. The McCanahan came after her, and at her whispered bidding, tilted the stone slab back into place. An instant before it fell, as his eyes were still above the floor level, he saw a man standing in the cell corridor, grinning at him.

The McCanahan almost cried out to Slyss.

The man in the cell corridor was burly, with black hair matted over his chest. He jangled a ring of keys at his side. It was Slib, the jailer, and his little eyes were clear and evil.

No man who lay drugged with wine ever boasted eyes like that! The only thing that troubled Kael was whether Slyss knew the jailer was awake and watching. If she knew, then he was being led into a trap, like a steer to the axing. If she did not know, then she was taking herself unwittingly into that same trap.

The McCanahan kicked off his buskins and walked with bare feet after the girl, along the cool damp floor of the sea vaults. In olden days, the primal men of Senorech had made their coves in these vaults to escape the ravening monsters of the dawn era. Here and there, in the light of the torches along the wall, he could see piles of white, bleached bones.

They walked for more minutes before he heard the faint rasp of metal touching rock.

Slyss was whirling, crying out.

From the shadows, men came leaping. As he plunged sideways, Kael noted that they were hardfaced Senn warriors. There was not a sfarran among them.

The McCanahan used his fist like a club, bringing its balled weight down in a full arm stroke, hitting the nearest man at the side of his neck, and driving him sideways into his companions. Before the man's falling club touched the floor, Kael held it, bringing it upward in a ceilingwise blow into the middle of the next man's belly.

Kael McCanahan had fought in the port taverns of Marsopolis and Dunverick. He had traded fists with Deneban dockwallopers and Karrvan stevedores. He knew every trick in the creeds of a dozen fighting races.

He used them all in the sea vaults below Akkalan. He used the club like a sword, driving it hard into a Senn's face. He hit backwards with it. He used an overhand, downward stroke, that drove the inches-long spikes that studded its knob, deep into a man's braincase.

It is no easy matter for ten men to cage one man. Not in dimly lighted pits, with that one man an explosive cyclone of fists and bashing club. Ten men keep getting in the way of each other. And Kael McCanahan was there to make each mistake a costly one.

He cut his opponents down to five in those first few minutes. Then he was at the wall, ripping loose the olisene-drenched torch, hurling it in their faces, to splatter in thick little globs of burning chemicals.

With their screams of pain ringing in the sudden darkness, the McCanahan slid forward into the blacker shadows. Out of sight he ran.

He found a tunnel that sliced at an angle into the main vault. He went along it, his bare feet making no sound.

He discovered another converging corridor and raced along that. Inside ten minutes, he lost himself in the labyrinthine vaults.

He came to a halt in the blackness, lungs gulping at cool air that was faintly spiced with seasalt. He listened, but heard no sound. When his heart ceased to thud so heavily against his ribs, he moved again. But now he went more cautiously, with the club before him like an overlong arm, probing the darkness.

He felt the cool updraft of air, just as his feet went out from under him.

CHAPTER VI

He slid for thirty feet on a wet ramp that dropped him flat on his back on the floor of a huge chamber lighted by radio-active filaments set flush to the stone walls. At the far end of the vast room, two mighty metal doors were hung on great bronze hinges.

On the floor of the room rested a hundred great daises. And on each dais lay a man or a woman.

"A tomb," the McCanahan muttered. "I've found one of the Senn burial chambers."

As he crawled to his feet and stared, he knew that this was no tomb. The bodies were flushed with life, and clad in the uniforms and trappings of a hundred different people. The McCanahan rubbed a bruised shoulder and went to walk among the daises.

A shepherd boy with a ragged sheepskin across his loins and over one shoulder, lay beside a trimly garbed officer of the Palace Guard. Beyond them, a silk-swathed dancing girl lay beside a heavily muscled halgor-driver, with the brown of the desert sun still on his forehead.

The McCanahan touched an arm. It was warm. It yielded beneath his fingers. He tried to rouse the man, without success.

A face in the third row over from the main aisle tugged at some chord of memory. He slipped between the daises, to stare down into the cold, haughty face of Captain Herms Borkus of the Fleet.

"Now would I had the wisdom of Bridget herself, the wisest woman in all Ireland," muttered the McCanahan. "Is this a store-room where the High Mor keeps those he has doomed to some punishment? Is it a place such as the visi-chambers on Vreer and Anafelm, where men and women spend most of their lives dreaming? And if it isn't any of these things, what in the name of the sons of Strongbow is it?"

He walked on, staring down at the faces of those who lay in this trance-like slumber. He saw a face or two he knew from remembered glimpses, in the days when he had walked the court of the High Mor as the son of the Terran Ambassador.

And then the McCanahan froze, and the blood in his veins moved with sluggish torpor.

Ahead of him, on the two largest daises of all, lay the twin bodies of the High Mor.

There was no mistake. He had seen that thin-lipped face too often where it leered down at Solar Command uniforms from the ruboid throne of Akkalan. The eyes were staring now, lifeless, but he remembered the scorn and the supreme contempt that had been in their depths.

The McCanahan was a baffled man.

He walked around the coffers, and his lips opened to speak, but no sound came out. "It's dreaming I am, with the little people flooding my brain with fancies from a fevered mind! The High Mor, twins—no, triplets!—for he must sit even now on the throne, dreaming up tortures for my body."

The creak of a door-hinge sent him to the floor.

He stared at the opening door, and smothered a curse in his throat when he saw the slave girl, Slyss of Aakan, glide into the room. She was alone. She went to an empty pier and lay upon her back.

And now the hair at the base of the McCanahan's neck stood straight up, for something was rising from all along her body. A something that was white and bright and dazzling, and from where he lay, Kael could feel the utter coldness of the thing.

"Noorlythin!" his numbed brain told him, and he hid his eyes.

He heard a faint tinkling, such a sound as he had heard once before, when he floated between the stars among the Doyen. He looked, and the swirling white radiance that was Noorlythin was settling down on one of the bodies of the High Mor, and the High Mor was sitting up, chafing at wrists and fingers, swinging his legs to the floor.

In the ancient legends of Terra, there was mention of an Arabic ruler, one Haroun al Raschid, who went in disguise among his people, that he might learn their thoughts and their way of living. It came to the McCanahan as he lay here that Noorlythin was such a one, but he used no simple disguises. He took the body of a man, or the body of a woman, and possessed it.

Kael retched silently, remembering the caresses he had given the slave girl. That *thing* had been inside her, controlling the pity in her eyes, the poses of her body. It had been Noorlythin who had led him into the vaults below the castle, for some reason he did not yet know. It had been Herms Borkus, seeking the secret of his harp. He knew now why the smashing of the tube in the great machine had not shut off his lack of motive power, as it had the robotlike bodies of the sfarran crew.

"By all the sand on Mars," the McCanahan gritted between his teeth, "I have a secret worth a thousand suns in my hand. But how can I best use it?"

The High Mor was at the huge doors now. He went out without a backward glance, and the doors slid shut behind him.

Kael came to his feet. He looked around him at the faces of the men and women who lay awaiting the coming of the Doyen. He knew what he had to do, and his face twisted in repugnance. Without these bodies, Noorlythin was trapped in the body of the High Mor; he was the High Mor, and no other. If these bodies were destroyed, smashed beyond recognition, Noorlythin could never use them, perhaps to appear again before the McCanahan in the guise of an officer or beautiful woman.

Kael gripped his club more firmly and walked slowly down the long rows of coffers. At each dais, he paused a little while and did what had to be done. Once he stripped a man and donned the uniform of the Senn Fleet, acquiring the rank of major.

He left Slyss until the last.

But when he stood there, looking down into that smooth face, eyeing the yellow hair that tumbled around the creamy shoulders, he could not nerve himself to the task at hand.

"I'll let her be. At least I know her as a cradle for Noorlythin. I'll be on my guard."

With a sword at his side and an addy-gun holstered to his service belt, the McCanahan dropped the club. He went to the doors and swung them open, and walked out into a long corridor hewn from living stone.

For nearly an hour he followed that corridor, travelling steadily upwards. He emerged into a palace guardroom whose rack-hung walls were filled with handguns and swords, with keen-edged axes and cloaks with the dragon of the Senn emblazoned on collar and breast.

And in the guard room, he found the High Mor waiting for him.

"It is better this way," said the High Mor. "Just the two of us, face to face. I thought it might be better, as Slyss, to lure you into a Senn trap, and then to pretend a rescue by my sfarran guards just as they were about to torture you. I thought I might claim your allegiance that way."

The McCanahan showed his teeth. "And after you'd wormed the truth of my secret weapon out of me, you'd hang me to a rack with the metal hooks biting into my naked back, and pull on my legs until the hooks came out. After that—"

The High Mor waved a hand.

"There is no need of torture between us, Terran. Oh, at first I wanted your life. Your father stumbled on a Senn scientist who discovered that a certain microwave shattered a peculiar type glass much used by the sfarri, due to sonic disturbances created in the atmosphere.

"Since the sfarri are a race of robots, created by the Doyen so long ago that were I to tell you the number of years involved they would be meaningless to you, they are necessarily energized by machines. In those machines a klyptric tube, made of that glass, forms an antennae that picks up and transmits the power generated by the machine. It broadcasts it in wave-lengths attuned to the internal structure of the sfarri."

"You tell me nothing new," Kael grated. "Most of that I learned myself from putting one and two and three together."

The High Mor threw back his jeweled cloak and rested a thigh on the edge of a gaming table. His eyes glittered brightly.

He said, "You are no fool, Terran. I do not underestimate you, believe me. I tell you this to explain why I felt it necessary to kill your father."

"And Captain Edmunds! And Cassy Garson! And all the men who were in the *Eclipse* when your sfarrans rayed her into a smoking ruin just outside the planetal orbit of Senorech!"

The High Mor gestured. His graceful white hands waved apology. "For all that, I am sorry. I made a mistake. Now I offer what I can to atone for my errors.

"Join me. Wear my dragon! To you, I promise such power as no man has ever dreamed. The wants of a Napoleon, or a Bral Kan of Procyon! Not even Gartillin Vo of Deneb, or Cygnis Hannon will outshine you in the splendor of your triumphs!

"Do you think I want to spend my time in this?" and here the High Mor gestured at his body. "I want to go back to the Temple of Sharrador where once I dwelt for many ages, worshipped and adored."

The McCanahan grinned. "You know I recognize you as Noorlythin?"

"You were in the chamber where I keep the bodies I use. I felt your presence."

Kael stared his surprise.

"I knew you watched," the High Mor went on. "I could have spoken to you there. But it is better to meet you this way, face to face, away from those reminders that I am not as you. In a humanoid body, I may speak with you, as man to man.

"Only this way can I hope to convince you that I offer you more than you can ever gain without me. I am no man. I am a god! A god of primal space! I have lived for eon piled upon eon, hunting and seeking through the stars, studying the worlds I found. On some I lived for ages, on others I dwelt for only a little while. All those worlds, Kael McCanahan, I offer you!

"Be an emperor, Terran! Rule every planet in all space. The greatest jewels of Strae'eth or Vrann can be yours, to wear on your person or to be hung in ropes of diamonds about the neck of any woman in all space! Lead my battle fleets! On distant Sfar, my technicians shall make you a hundred billion sfarrans to serve under your banner. They shall make the greatest warships that ply the starlanes, each one encrusted with your name!"

The McCanahan shivered. It was a prospect that shook a man loose from his moorings.

To rule the stars! To sit on a throne and gaze out at the peoples of the universe bowed before him. To have the faery women of Cygni and Flormaseron in a harem, waiting his pleasure.

It was a thought that would have appealed to nine men in ten. Kael McCanahan called himself a fool, but he turned his visions aside.

"I want no conquests. I want no jewels. The only woman I want is Flaith. Where is she?"

The High Mor sighed. "In a tower, well guarded. No harm has come to her. No harm will come. I am no sadist to harm a woman. Not when what I seek is possessed by a man. Tell me, Terran. What is your price?"

"Peace! Friendship with Terra and the men of Terra. Let the Solar Combine send its traders to Senorech. Peace between the peoples of the stars."

The High Mor laughed. "I too, seek peace. A peace that will end with my dragon banner floating above the towers of New Washington, Terra. With your precious Solar Combine run by the sfarri. I offer you a place in that peace, Kael McCanahan. A high place. The highest place of all! I am a god! I have no need of earthly things. You do.

"Give me your answer, Terran!"

For a moment, the temptation was there. But in that same moment, the McCanahan remembered the blasted *Eclipse*, and the dead Father he loved, and Captain Edmunds, straight and lean in his white Fleet uniform. A memory came to him of Cassy Garson and the kisses she had given him in a drifting galley on the Tigranian Sea. The High Mor was not human. He knew nothing of the loves and lusts, the fears and terrors of human beings. He was as far removed from the Senn and Terrans as man is from the ant.

"I answer—no! You'd blacken Earth with your rays and leave empty ruins. You'd take everything in space! And me—what of me?"

The High Mor smiled. "You would rule the universe!"

But Kael McCanahan shook his head stubbornly. "I cannot believe that. If I once tell you—"

Beware, Terran!

The Doyen thought warned him just in time.

The High Mor brought his hand out from under his cloak and he held a black-metal stinger in his fingers. It spat a stream of violent fire at the McCanahan.

Kael dove sideways. The tip of his finger slipped through the violet fire and it stung with the agony of seared nerve-ends. If full effect of that blast had touched him he would be writhing helplessly on the floor, his body one gigantic mass of pain.

He had seen the stinger turned on unregenerate killers. It softened them in a hurry.

His shoulder hit the edge of the table where the High Mor sat. The table upended, and the High Mor fell to the floor with him.

Kael put a hand to the throat of the other man and his fingers tightened and squeezed. It was like choking a bar of steel. The High Mor forced a laugh through his lips, and his body twisted like an uncoiling spring and forced the McCanahan from him.

"The Doyen warned you. I caught the thought they put in your brain! Well, let them play their game. They can only interfere with me when I use my Doyen powers to destroy you. I have other gifts to use!"

A fist dove at his face, but the McCanahan was a master at rough and tumble fighting. He slipped it and bored in. His fists drummed into the High Mor's belly, lifted and threw him back to rebound off the far wall.

A dozen weapons came tumbling down on the ruler of Senorech. A cloak swathed his flailing arms.

Kael stepped back, waiting.

That was where he made his mistake. For the High Mor slid to the floor in a crumpled heap, and the thing that was Noorlythin glowed and pulsed and moved its frosted tendrils, free of its fallen body.

As Noorlythin moved its tendrils, the floor fell away beneath the booted heels of the McCanahan. The walls of the guardroom went out of existence, and Kael was falling, falling.

Gird yourself, Terran! You go into subspace where no other living thing can enter! Not even another Doyen to shield you from my wrath! For each Doyen has in him the seeds of material creation, and what one Doyen materializes, no other Doyen can disturb!

And the high, mocking laughter followed him down and down, into the eternal blackness where he fell.

CHAPTER VII

A hot sun blanketed his naked body. It blazed from a molten sky and cooked him where he lay on warm red rocks. Kael McCanahan lifted his head and stared at the searing desolation before him. Sand and rock, and the shale of evaporated seas, stretching like the finger of Time to infinity itself, outward to that blazing blue bowl of sky where the golden sun hung high, pouring down its heat.

He came to his feet and swayed with the pain that the heat was putting in his muscles.

Come to me! Come! Come!

He put trembling hands to his head, and again that sweet call sounded, with the siren lure of all the lost treasures of all space.

He stumbled forward, hearing the summons in his brain, in every fibre of his being.

Come to my riches! Lift up your hands to the jewel that gives man everything he wants! Touch me! I am yours!

He was running across the hot sands that bit his naked feet with hot teeth, and over the sharp rocks that cut into his flesh until he bled. Dimly, he knew that nothing could help him now. That here he was cut off from everything that was sane.

This mad world was a creation of Noorlythin. His was the wild brain that dreamed the sands and the rocks and the awful desolation. His dream, that sun that cooked while it shone.

Sobbing, he ran. He fell to his knees, and he crawled.

With bleeding fingers he clawed at the rocks, making himself rise and run again.

It seemed to the man that had once been Kael McCanahan that he was running around a planet. The pain was part of him, now. His muscles jerked in agony at every step, yet always he forced himself to run faster, faster, gulping down the hot desert air. That siren call was strong in his ears.

Run, Terran! Run to me!

He ran on and on, and now he saw the others, men like himself, running on bleeding feet, crawling when those feet were worn to cracked stumps. And before each of those men, or before Kael McCanahan's own eyes, gleamed—

The eye of Lirflane!

A globe of a red jewel it was, the eye. Imprisoned in its faceted surface were the dreams of a billion people. The man that looked on it saw the happiness he sought, and he fought to join himself to it, that his own dreams would add to the total of all the others. And on the dreams and on the flesh of these men who came to it, drawn by its siren voice and by the eternity of delight it promised, the eye of Lirflane feasted, waxed and swelled.

A man tried to claw at his legs as Kael McCanahan ran past him. Red eyes in a bloated face hurled hate at him, as his hand closed on his ankle.

The McCanahan shook himself free and ran on.

The eye was closer now.

It grew massive, transparent. In its redness, the redness of the hair of flaming Flaith beckoned. Her white body swayed and danced, and her throaty voice summoned him.

The McCanahan's arms shook as he put them out, trying to pull himself forward with handfulls of hot, desert air.

Now the Eye of Lirflane was before him, and all he could see was Flaith moving toward him, her arms wide and beckoning—

One step he moved, and another.

His hand went out, toward the gleaming red side of the monstrous jewel.

Come to me, Kael McCanahan! Come to the peace and the forgetfulness you have earned. Take me in your arms. Drink kisses from my lips!

The McCanahan sobbed.

He shook in torture more vivid than the agony in his feet and muscles.

"Not Flaith!" he cried. "Not Flaith! You—woman of the jewel! Witchwoman of Lirflane! Not Flaith!"

He went to his knees, to anchor himself the better to the ground, against the siren call of the mighty Eye.

"No. Got to fight! Get free. Free...."

He fought there on his knees, while men streamed past him, rushing with insane desire into the red heaven of the jewel. Their eyes were mad with the greed or the lust that shook them, for every man saw in the Eye of Lirflane what his own eyes wanted most to see. Their bodies were torn and gaunt from their struggle across the sand and rock desolation. But they would lose their pain, within the bosom of the red eye.

Kael fought. He fought silently, until the sweat came out on his face in big globes, until it runneled down his chest and thighs. His belly and his back were awash with the salt dampness.

At last he turned, just a little, so that only a corner of the fabulous Eye remained in his vision.

An hour later, he turned again, and now he saw only the barren loneliness of this abandoned world. And as he stared, the sand and the rocks and the sky ran with liquid movement as a painting might run in a bath of chemicals. And the streaming reds and buffs and yellows, the black and the greens and purples flowed together and formed a river, that swept the tortured legs of the McCanahan out from under him.

He screamed in his agony as the salt water bit into his bleeding wounds. He babbled and twisted, flailing the salt sea with animal desperation. He drowned in this vast emptiness of ocean, with no hand to grasp his or eye to witness his going.

"No," he shouted to the gray leaden sky above him. "I won't die! I'll live! I'll live!"

His arms and his legs moved, and clumsily, he swam. No driftwood floated here. Here a man had to swim to stay alive, until his arms and his legs grew numb with his effort, and he sank.

The McCanahan turned on his back, and the salt water buoyed him up. He floated for endless days, and during endless nights, and the tiny spark of life within him waxed and waned. And out of the eternity of no-time, as he swam and alternately floated, a wing-prowed galley slipped through the foam-crested waves. Its white sail bellied in the ocean wind. It veered and came for him, running easily in the water.

From the rail, a bearded face scowled down at him. A hairy hand threw a rope that he twisted around his middle. He was dragged on deck, to stand dripping with the salt water that seared his wounds.

A rope was whipped around his wet wrists and he was dragged to the slim mast that rose from the deck, before the oarbanks where slaves pulled at smooth-handled oars.

A woman whose flesh was tinted a delicate green came toward him. She walked with quick, supple strides, and the McCanahan noted numbly that her eyes were a feral green, and that her tiny ears were pointed. A whip coiled in her hand.

She showed her tiny teeth in a cruel smile.

"You are the man from Terra! You are the one who turned down all the worlds of space! For that you must be punished!"

And the long lash went snaking out in an arc, slashing into his back, and the sheer agony of the cutting whip slammed his body against the mast. The lash came down and lifted, came down and lifted, and the McCanahan sagged in the ropes that held him.

With the cruelty of her species, the cat-woman flogged him. When she was done, she cut him loose and stood over him on the swaying deck that was stained with his blood. Her voice was soft, furry.

"Take him and chain him to an oar! Rivet the manacles on his wrists and ankles! Let him tug an oar for a year! Then perhaps he will obey Him who is ALL!"

He was kicked and shoved across the deck. He tumbled into an empty slot on an oarbench. His wrists and ankles were shackled, the armorer not caring where his metal mallet fell.

For a day he rested, with black bread soaked in wine forced between his teeth. For a day, he knew only the blessedness of not moving. His slumber was dreamless—

In a red dawn, he was wakened by the bite of an overseer's whip across his bloody back. His hands lifted and went to the oar-handle, and his body swayed and returned, and he put his weight with the weight of the men who held the same oar as he.

The galley slipped through the heaving ocean, and the red oars flashed in the sun, and the salt spray stung, and only when an errant wind swept across the seas was there any rest for the men who slaved on the benches. Sometimes men died, and were flung overboard. Other men were unshackled and dragged screaming to the foredeck, where the cat-woman waited, pink tongue licking her lips, the whip curling like a live thing in her hands.

And of all the men who worked the oars in this endless ocean, it was the McCanahan who was chosen most often for her amusement.

Once he almost died under the biting whip, and in that moment of pain and numbness, when his senses seemed about to float from his body, the cat-woman leaned close and her furry voice whispered, "Speak your secret to me, man of Terra! Tell me the weapon that slays the sfarri!"

But the McCanahan only shook his head and his hair, long uncut, tumbled on his bleeding shoulders.

The days were endless on that ocean, and the oars swung and the sail creaked, flapping overhead, and the overseer tramped the runway with endless patience, his voice a sullen growl. The cat-woman came to look upon the McCanahan and her slim greenish fingers came forth to stroke his naked back where her lash had marred it. Always her throaty voice whispered to him, speaking of the delights that might be found in her cabin, if only he were not so stubborn.

When her patience was at an end, she motioned to the overseer and he came with armed guards and unchained the McCanahan, and he was led to the mast and roped.

And then, in the middle of a whipsting, the ocean and the ship and the cat-woman's whip fell away....

He lay on a hard, cold floor.

The High Mor stood before him, his hard eyes glittering. Kael was back in the guardroom that he had left—how long ago?

"A year," said the High Mor, reading his thought. "A year and five days! And yet, the barest split second of Time. I sent you out to those worlds of subspace, Kael McCanahan. There you lived, and almost died. You rowed at a real oar. You suffered the cuts of a real whip. Look at yourself!"

The High Mor threw a small metal mirror at him. Dazedly he stared at the grim, hard brown face and the cold blue eyes he saw mirrored on its surface. His flesh was brown, and great muscles swelled under it. The oar had put those muscles there, as the whip had put the scars on his ribs and back.

"Only a split second of our time, Terran," said the High Mor. "But a year and five days in the worlds I made! I told you I had gifts! I have made a thousand million worlds for that subspace, in the eons that I have roamed the stars. I am a god!"

Kael shook his head and his long hair flicked his naked arms. If he needed proof of the High Mor's words, his long-uncut hair was proof enough.

He thought, *Tell him, and let him have his way! How can a man fight god?* The thought washed over him that he fought for all mankind, that the men and women of a thousand planets unknowingly depended on his fight. Women like the flame-tressed Flaith, men like his father and Captain Edmunds, who did their duty and died for it, all depended on what he did

He had to think, to go over this logically. What would be the thought processes of a god? A god was no mere mortal, to be judged and weighed by human wants and failings. In it there was no mercy, no thought for anything but itself.

Kael pushed himself away from the floor to stand on long brown legs.

Courage, man of Terra! He shall not trap you so again!

The Doyen voice gave him heart, but the High Mor sneered.

"I heard it, too, Terran! The Doyen cannot help you. Not unless I strive by Doyen means to kill you. I need not do that, Kael McCanahan, need I?"

The McCanahan shook his head like a dumb animal. He would never go back to that subspace where Noorlythin was a god in truth! To that hell, where a second was a year, where the Doyen themselves could not enter!

"I could put you there again, Terran. I could forget you, let you live out your life for an eternity of seconds that are years! Would you listen to reason then? Would you like to test your will again against that of the Eye of Lirflane? Or feel once more the lash of Vigrette, the cat-woman? No, I read in your eyes that you would not!

"Come, then. Tell me how you made the sfarri die!"

Speak, man of Terra! Tell Noorlythin what he seeks! Only then, as he absorbs the knowledge, can we reach him!

The McCanahan shrugged the great shoulders that were scarred with the lash above the smooth roll of their bulging muscles. His head hung so that his uncut hair shielded his face.

"The harp," he whispered. "On the harp of Brith Tsinan is a silver string. The d-note! I strung it with a silvern wire that I loosed from my father's wrist!"

And as he spoke, he moved.

As liquid as the falling waters in the Veil of Valmoora was the leap of the McCanahan. Full into the High Mor he hurtled, knocking him sideways. And as they went down together—

The Doyen struck!

The very rocks of the palace misted and swirled under that awesome itching. White fire flared and seared, and where it touched, all matter was destroyed! The walls of the palace shook and quivered. Beams groaned under the sudden stress.

Where the guardroom had been, was empty nothingness!

In a flame that lapped him protectingly as it flared fiercely and strongly at Noorlythin himself, the Doyen carried both men upward. So swift was their transmission through normal space that in one blinding surge of the white flame, the McCanahan found himself between the worlds, in some lost, dark blotch of empty space.

"No Doyen may slay another Doyen!"

That voice rang triumphantly in the abyss.

"There is a way, Noorlythin! That is why we have let you work your will on this man. He hates you with a deadly hate, Noorlythin. You put him in your worlds of subspace, and you abandoned him to the creatures of your own creation!"

"Aie! I abandoned him! Were it not for him and his harp, I would reign as a god on every planet in all inhabited space. The Solar Combine would have fallen to my sfarran battle fleet!"

"You dared not move before you knew the one weapon that might defeat you!"

"Now I know! Now! Now!"

The radiant energy in the thing that was Noorlythin was awful. It beat and flared redly through the whiteness. The McCanahan shuddered as its heat beat out at him, chilling even as it seared.

Courage, Terran! Courage for what lies ahead!

And now the voices shrank and whispered, piping like elfin horns within his head, that none but he could hear.

Through you, we may destroy him! Courage! With your help, he dies—forever!

He knew what he had to do. Of his free will he had to offer himself to Noorlythin! Of his free will, he had to fling himself into the mad embrace of those pulsing tendrils, that had turned Lunol the peddler to black and drifting dust!

He gave you to the Eye of Lirflane! He gave you to the cat-woman and her whip!

The McCanahan snarled. "Destroy him, and I save the Solar Combine! I hear you, Doyen. I hear and I—obey!"

And Kael McCanahan flung himself headlong, forward into the white whirlwind of force that was Noorlythin.

In the Chamber of Living Death, she who had been Slyss of Aaka quivered fitfully. A bubble of froth broke from her red lips. She moane and stirred. A hand lifted, struggled feebly, fell back to her side, limp and waxen.

Slyss opened brown eyes. She lay silent, staring upward at the ceiling. A sob fought its way upward from her throat.

"Noorlythin is dead! His control over me and the others—gone forever!"

She rolled off the dais and stared around her, at the dead bodies. She shivered. She went to the doors and pulled them open. In the distance, she could hear the frightened roaring of terrified men. She began to run.

Flaith shook the bars of the cell that held her. Her red hair made a living flame about her shoulders.

"What is happening? What is it?" she screamed.

A terrified jailer paused in his heavy run past her cell.

"The palace is falling in! The High Mor is dead. His body has been found!"

Flaith shook the barred door.

"Let me out! Please, please! Give me a chance to save myself!"

The jailer licked his lips. He glanced up and down the corridor, then slid the key into the lock. The door opened under a push from his hand. "If the High Mor is dead," he told the girl, "maybe the sfarri won't stay here on Senorech! Maybe the Senn can rule themselves, now."

Flaith caught the man by his arm.

"The one I was captured with! Kael McCanahan, the Earther! Where is he?"

"Nobody knows! His cell is empty."

"His harp? Man, where is his harp?"

The jailer shook himself free and started down the corridor. Over his shoulder he called, "Look in the storehouse beyond the cell block. We keep all prisoners' effects in there!"

Terran! Wake to life, Kael McCanahan!

He was dead. He had thrown himself into the fiery maw of the thing that was Noorlythin. Who called him now? Who spoke these lies?

You live, Terran. You served as the catalyst that enabled us to focus our powers against Noorlythin.

Even a high school student knew that a catalyst retained its own identity during the chemical change it brought about between two substances; even such substances as were the Doyen, gods of space.

Kael opened his eyes.

He lay on a floor in the wreckage of the guardroom in the palace of Akkalan. In the distance, but growing closer, he heard the faint strumming of harpstrings. He lay there and listened to the harp, as life flowed stronger into his body.

The strumming came nearer.

The McCanahan stood up and he waited, big and brown, marked with scars.

Flaith stood in the broken doorway, her fingers falling from the harp. Tears had formed twin channels from her red-lashed eyes along her cheeks. When she saw Kael, she did not know him. And then he grinned, and his long hair and scarred brown body were forgotten.

She flung herself at him, and lay against him, trembling.

He told her of the High Mor and what he had been, and of how the Doyen had destroyed him. "We've won, Flaith. He's dead, forever. With the harp—and the vibrators that we'll build to duplicate its pitch—the Solar Combine will move on Sfar. Smash it, and its robot life!"

Laughter bubbled in her throat as she looked up at him. "They'll reward you, Kael. Make you somebody big on Terra!"

The McCanahan grinned and hugged her.

"An admiral at least! How would you like to be wed to an admiral, Flaith mavourneen?"

Her answer rocked him, in the hunger of her mouth on his.